necropolis

necropolis

jill alexander essbaum

foreword by
JILL PELÁEZ BAUMGAERTNER

neoNuma ARTS
HOUSTON, TX

neoNuma Arts
P.O. Box 460248
Houston, TX 77056

www.neonuma.com

Library of Congress Control Number: 2008929659

ISBN: 978-0-9741623-4-8

All poems copyright Jill Alexander Essbaum
Foreword copyright Jill Peláez Baumgaertner

All scripture passages are from the Kings James Version of the Bible.

Cover and title page illustration created by Misha Penton from photos by Dave Nickerson. www.artbymisha.com

...chiefly for Nick Cave.

Hast thou entered into the springs of the sea? Or hast thou walked in the search of the depth? Have the gates of death been opened unto thee? Or hast thou seen the doors of the shadow of death? Hast thou perceived the breadth of the earth? Declare if thou knowest it all.

Job 38: 16-18

contents

Foreword   xi

Introit   1

I. The First Day

On the First Day   5
Necropolis   6
Terra Infirma   8
Early Morning Prayer   10
The Great Undertaking   11
Madame Fortuna Surveys Your Here and Your After   12
What We Did   15
Cemetery Road   16
Surely You're Dead, We Eulogized You   17
Buried   19
Hotel Infinity   20
Threnody   21
A Wish   22
Houses, Haunted   23
A Good Christian Mustn't Fear the Darkness of the Grave   25

II. The Second Day

On the Second Day   29
Epitaph   30
Vesper   31
Danse Macabre   32
What We Didn't   33
The Lord Summons His Regret   34
New Jerusalem   35
A Razor to the Throat Ought to Do It—   36
Gethsemane   38
A Little Song   39
Postmark from Gehenna   40
What (C)remains   41
An Alabaster Jar and its Oil   42
Once Was I   43
A Funerary Catechism   44
The Question is One of Ashes and Dust   45

As One Crying Out in the Wilderness   46

III. The Third Day

On the Third Day   51
Variety of Hells   52
What Death Makes of You   53
An Ache like a Stone   55
These Last Things (Lest I Forget Them)   56
Cross   57
La Petite Mort   58
Cinerary Song   59
The things they don't tell you about heaven   60
Says Some Angel to One Mary or Another—   61
Mount   62
RSVP   65
If We Meet Again   66
The Naming of Things   67
Deathday   68
Last Day   69
O Afterwards: A Benediction   70

Notes and Acknowledgements   73

foreword

ONE OF THE MOST CHALLENGING PARTS of writing my father's funeral eulogy was using past tense verbs to refer to one so recently alive that he was still present. So Jill Alexander Essbaum, in poem after poem, struggles in this remarkable collection with the death of her mother, which reminds her, in so many inescapable ways, of her own endings. An undertone throughout the first section is Christ's Good Friday suffering and burial, entwined and enmeshed with all of the other losses. In each one's death is the other's.

She does not flinch in her steady gaze at the tomb and at the dissolution of the body. Even though "a sun is wasted in the sky," the "clocks tick bravely forward" anyway, taking her to the second day, Holy Saturday, when Christ is most deeply dead, the sun is silent, and the speaker is edgy and questioning. "How exactly has your will been done?" she asks as she learns to live in the grey areas of ambiguity where belief and doubt exist simultaneously.

There is no magic resolution, no crazy joy on the third day, the traditional day of Christ's resurrection. Instead, Essbaum writes, "What death makes of you is, simply, a mess./ And it's no matter whether you're the griever or the one/ who's grieved. You're stiff, stifled, stalled." The questions permeate this section as she also envisions judgment and last things along with resurrection, God "knitting once again my limbs to my skin." Still, she asks, will sin or grace win?

This collection avoids facile answers and grapples with the

hard reality that when we need him most, God is often most silent. Jill Essbaum is the questioner, as persistent and faithful as Job, hoping finally that she may "turn to gold" but aware always that from ashes we have come and to ashes we will return.

JILL PELÁEZ BAUMGAERTNER
Poetry Editor, *The Christian Century*
Dean of Humanities and Theological Studies,
Wheaton College

introit

I was dead and I went for a walk this morning.
        Dead, long dead, and I went out for a walk.

I rose from the bed like Lazarus from his tomb,
        like a debutante iris bulbing towards Original

Bloom, like a tongue lapping the roof
        of my own mouth's cave. Fresh from the grave,

I rattled down wet streets where once I lived,
        streets now so serene, I presupposed them

deep in prayer, even as the supplicating ache
        of early day priested me along the aisles

of this queer, black church, this silent dread,
        down to the altar of my fate. So be the deadweight

despair that certain darkness brings, the knowing
        that you *were* and no more *are*. Long dead,

I was well past tense, and on my way to panic
        and still I walked, stalking the misplaced slice

of evidence, scheming the piece of the whole
        damn pie. *How did I die?* I couldn't recall.

The sky was unaccommodating. Above,
        a slim, single rib of lifeless light as the moon's

feeble crescent waned closed. Below,
        the pavement seemed to know me by my bare,

bereaving steps. So I urged, naked as a lover
        or a corpse, through the hour of 5 A.M., a solemn awe

sustaining me while the living city slept
        so unperturbedly at ease, that strange, comatose

sleep of libertines and fools: the clear conscience
        of unconsciousness from which repose even nightmares

cannot rouse. I suffered beneath the still of it
        as Christ under Pilate endured his defeat. *And what*

of me was ever really true? I shammed
        through my days like a bon vivant. *And who*

is ever truly dead? The houses stood as I
        remembered them, on crisp, square plots,

in sane, straight rows, and each belittling lawn
        damp with dawn. Houses that had haunted me

as I now haunted them. The duplex where I learned
        duplicity. The gingerbread house which furnished

its very own witch and a hush-hush cupboard abundant
        with puddings and ants. The sergeant's house. The wife's.

The house of the eight inch pearl-handled knife.
        The loft where far ago I idled through nights in alien

arms of men whose names I've buried
        and I'll never disinter. The last, black house

which wore my only gloom like a saint's
        hair shirt. No one could have sinned my sins but me.

The stains I shamed on bedsheets. How I seeped
        like a miracle hand, how and who I stigmatized,

exactly ecstatic. These crimes were mine alone
        and I draped them like a pall over bones I'd before festooned

in the silly rag of flesh that was my skin.

        And that's as good a place as any to begin.

the first day

> *My heart is sore pained within me:
> and the terrors of death are fallen upon me.*
> Psalm 55:4

> *My face is foul with weeping,
> and on my eyelids is the shadow of death;
> not for any injustice in mine hands: also my prayer is pure.*
> Job 16:16-17

on the first day

They put him in the ground as if hiding
a great treasure. An ox-sized boulder marked
the spot of it, and a crown of thistle.
Women shined their faces with tears. Friday
grew colder than ever it was meant for.
Peter suggested it was time to leave,
and many of the people left. Some stayed
to pray and to mourn. Others watched the sky
for a sign like a star. Day dimmed nightly,
and the moon showed herself on the tomb's roof
dancing like Bathsheba, naked and round,
full as a living body. Dreams survived
the watchers through those hard hours, foretelling
calm and its calamity. Jesus slept.

necropolis
> *See, I have set before thee this day life and good, and death and evil...*
> Deuteronomy 30:15

Neither is it beyond the sea, for it is
    too shallow. Neither is it in heaven,

where thrones carouse the feet of God,
    oh order of angels awaiting. Neither

is it the life you are given, *born into,*
    the life you neither earn nor deserve.

Neither is it the bladder of muscle once
    you called The Heart. Fuller than most,

she's emptied now, erupted. Neither
    is it the fume of volcanic simile, but see

here: *The lava leaps hotly like a hundred*
    suns, dancing. It is not the cause

of a Christian to pray as the pagans pray,
    your hands black as a secret's unknowing

ease. Not in your hands at all. It's nothing
    you have ever loved, or said you loved.

Neither Adam nor apple, nor anyone's
    business but Christ's. It isn't the City

of Sleep, insensibly thrumming its slumber.
    Suffering's only cure is ignorance.

It is no longer in you to be ignorant.
    It isn't the gate to the lamb shack,

so far away, so damn divine. It is
    not the grief incurred lingering within

an absent man's shade. Too long
        have you waited. Still, he is not here.

Oh, Soul. The price of life is death.

terra infirma

Through demon and through deity,
      under seventeen or seven thousand years,
      the mountain before you appears
to be smiling. Circumstantially,

the evidence supports this by a crack,
      wide and scheming in the old hill's hull,
      the sinister grin it assumes. The chasm swells
as a virgin might. Within, a black,

wet warmth suspends itself as if some ancient
      orgasm died here of defeat, its form still swinging
      from the rope what hung it, successfully deceased.
No. That's not quite sorrow enough. Try this:

You're dead, deserted, desolate. This landscape
      is everything Loss. Through devilment,
      through destiny, no sly, bright star will mount
into a optimistic sky, no plain shine of day

shall ever unfurl its rosy curl. Instead,
      it is the let-down of a waited-for awake. You're
      not to be roused nor risen again. Austere
is the outlook. And that, my Pet, is how death

disappoints, forsakes. Trumpetless,
      the unappealing air will never bell.
      And every last deed you feated, Jezebel,
arrived you at this place of final rest.

Does it surprise you, how quiet the scenery
      seems? Prepare yourself. The mountain's
      mouth will squall out its chorus of moans
when it pleases. Grim symphony,

it is a thunder-pang arranged for many voices.
      Dead fathers make the most noise here,
      for even their darling daughters have disappeared,
lost beyond the bastard canyon's choke. And Jesus says

Pray Always. It's best you do as he intones.
        Into this gorge goes cities, goes sleep.
        It does not waste its pity on the vagrant or his queen.
The veil's been lifted. The white light foams.

An everlasting night divides by time,
        but your hours are over. Infinity inflames.
        Deliver any mercies you can congregate.
Lover: There is nothing left of Christ.

early morning prayer

This watch is set for imaginary time,
the schedule of physicist's dreams
and the inventive sighs of sleepy men

with erections. At this present, my heart
is in its heap as a streetlight flickers against
fickle shadows and a late neighbor

whistles for his dog. At five or so
in the morning, my shivering legs
are famous, and my fingers grieve

their lover's talents. At five or so
in the morning, I have learned
the aftermath of lying awake

and living it is little deaths, one
upon the other, stacked like bodies
making love. Oh God, how I pray

that you are better, not bigger
than I thought. You are impending
enough at this misshapen hour.

the great undertaking

Coffin derives from French for 'little basket,' but caskets are square. An amateur's mistake. Neveryoumind, my humdrum bunny. Let us paint your Easter face. Golden, you ask? That's simply your gilt. The damask rose revenges its own wreath, I like to say. But like a pinwheel in a vase, you'll find fresh ways to rattle where you're planted, I'm convinced. Oh, there will be sorrow. Full decanters of sad will be wailed. Friends will lay down lilies. Won't it be swell? That's nice. Lie quiet. The draining's near completed. Are you relieved? I thread judicious seals in every orifice and valve. Last words? I'll next be sewing shut your pout. Out-and-out lovely, the fasten of your mouth. I should have liked to kiss it. This won't take long. And soon, you'll be a hidden thing. The Empress of Red Ants, indeed! Or, perhaps they'll crown you King? Forgive. These days, I scarcely bother making sure. So many disembodies, I'm best kept preserving this sexless decorum (lest I conjure novel breeds of old taboos). Poor bones, it's cold down where you're going. You're likely to catch fright, neither lamp nor match to strike, and quartered in the bastard dark, alone. But my hullabaloo here is done. No more tactless swellings in your every limb and love. No, wait. There's this. I've one last gift. A parting souvenir, we'll call it. No consolation. A penny for luck, the ferryman's fare. Though beg a final pardon. Was your name good or god?

madame fortuna surveys your here and your after

It's not yet out of your hands, the matter.
      We shall endeavor then, by reading the flat or

the fiat of your palm and *let it be done:*
      You will traipse toward these strange terrains of Zion

fingering the only atlas that Destiny's
      diagrammed. The Index is the key.

See? From the base of the ridge to its conical tip,
      it points out the highlights along this trip,

of which, the Lunar Mount is first.
      Hmmm. These moony hillocks seem to infer

Depressive leanings. Tell me, in the old life, did you
      often wane and wax? How frequent were the blue

dog's attacks, his wolfbane teeth
      at ease

in your chest? The sign points to this:
      You were come and go sad, now and then amiss.

Move along. We've other destinations. Erosions impede
      the uppermost trail. The fork in the plain speaks

plainly: Soul-sore and aching, you longed as a compass
      for Absolute North. This did not pass,

and thrust faults furrowed in your reservoirs,
      veering to those places your heart's glacier

ablated. I'm sensing that it scraped over outlooks it oughtn't
      have razed. But the days of your knuckles' wrought-

iron knots are done. On the farther coast, Mercury's
      beach, a whole deserted landslip wrecked by that Sea

of All Feeling wherein Too Much was always felt.
    Under those breakers, you dwelt,

hapless and hoping for the tides to swell
    to gold. The peninsula of the thumb forestalls

for measures of dexterity. *Have you any?*
    So concurs the fate-line: *A phalanx of catastrophes*

have come, have gone, will come again. They roost,
    an omen of rooks in the krummholz, aroused

by the decades of your travails. Wifely,
    you lived a good life, mostly.

Your meridians were straight as arrows, your nails,
    well-bedded in their own, the vale

of your virtue, bare of lustful leas. *Please.*
    It is appointed but once for a woman to rest in her peace,

and it's best to tell the truth, nothing but. Where a transverse
    byway rides *Via Lascivia*, it cautions a dearth of yearnings,

both prim and perverse. The highway itself, an overdeveloped drive:
    scenic, fleeting, concretized—

shall I go on? I predict a journey undertaken.
    Regard, a certain southbound trench. It slakes

from the center of your hand to your wrist and flumes
    to a flourish in the valley where chrysanthemums bloom,

where lilies lie right in repose.
    This is the river you've yet to roam.

A watershed moment, this break in the line,
    for it marks with a handspan scar the night

that you died. That very night, the last of last goodbyes. Before
    you, acres of waves furl out in whorls.

Behind you, the prints your foot left latently.
    Atop you, sediment only.

Your only lifeline's been untied,
    and the beckoning channel is deep, is wide.

It's no use asking was your soul
    worth saving. That's not for you to know.

The closet where you used to pray is closed.
    It's begging time. Eternity unfolds.

And, like a roadmap out of its glovebox,
    you cannot easily recrease it. Epochs

and eras will pass away. Your deeds won't be remembered,
    and everything you loved or touched will cinder

to ash underground. Grieve not for your bones
    and the quarry of flesh they home in. I forebode

a woman on the other shore. *Do you see her?*
    Black Sara looms to lay her dress upon the waters.

You will not founder nor drown. These depths run profoundly.
    Don't look down.

For shadow moves as sun commands it, darkly.
    Oh my dear, dead darling,

the surf, though heaving, is lovely
    enough, warm and thin as the tea my telling leaves

swim in,
    well-suited as kidskin

to the fashion of your fingers and each ring.
    Gypsy, no more shall you go a-wandering.

By consequence of God, your kismet attends.
    The end of all rivers implores: *Get In.*

what we did

We rode the wreck of our Adventure to Oratory Island,
said some poems there. We did it in the lock-bin
of the ice truck. Cold, but our bones forgave us
their freeze. We triumphed over treacheries of rain.
We swelled like tides, breathed as animals might.

You held me like a champion woodchopper handles
his axe. The highland's white phlox and hemlock
sang out *fierce, fierce joy*. Under the firs, a pungency
of grass and tussock. I said *lover* and you felt
for the diadem, beneath.

We wept in circles when the moonrise failed.
We prayed each other's Rosary. We laughed
that our callings were missed, a little ruined.
Priestly enough, water was turned into even brighter
water. In a priestly way, we lamented our bodies before us.

cemetery road

I walk through the city as if in my sleep
but the road sobers me. On the left,
an unlocked gate and graves in disrepair.
I hear the shambling away of sinister footfalls.
I smell the char of an untended fire.
Behind the very last of many broken headstones,
a fig tree. Wooden. Bare.

The soil is like glass when I touch it. A sun
is wasted in the sky. From this tree, learn its lesson:
For fruit that feeds and grows full in imminent
sunlight, there are other harvests germinating
in darkness, equally impending. Out from the earth
comes good things to eat. Wise in the ground,
good things are eaten away.

Into hands unknown, my spirit is condemned.
I will grow into a black pear, globular
and entwined by long tendrils and a cardioclast sorrow.
A vinedresser will cut away what might have been
my bounty. He will feed me to his animals.
Wild wheat and christ-thorn will spring up
from my burned and bitter seeds.

surely you're dead, we eulogized you

Now, ladies from your church bring casseroles
    and folding chairs. So we eat and we sit,

chitting small chat of death. You are not here,
    but none can say for certain where exactly

you've gone. *A better place*, the general
    consensus, where presently, your wrecked breath

affords some queenly mansion, where your soul
    has sloughed its unsympathetic shell,

like a python weeps away its winter
    skin. Indeed, that's the heaven we're hoping

you're in. Those who disabuse this logic
    do so quietly, and to themselves. For

isn't speculation how we best traverse
    the hard landscape of grief? *And wasn't it*

a lovely service, all the way around?
    There are lilies in every blue corner

of your house. Lilies atop the piano
    dirging fresh hymns to no one's tune,

lilies in the living room and living
    (what nerve!), as if to simply prove to you

it can, by fact, be done. There are lilies
    in your kitchen, where, one by one by one,

long-forgotten cousins refill coffee
    mugs and marvel to each other how many

years it's been, and *Let's not keep so far*
    apart again. Even are there lilies

on your bed. Surely you are dead. If not,
    perhaps we just misplaced you and forgot

where last you lay? One stormy Easter Sunday,
    I hid the eggs inside. It took three weeks

of rotting to remind me that I left
    the last one propped behind a hanging picture

frame. Today, I hunted down the walls,
    I dragged through drawers, I searched the sheets —

you are nowhere I can see. Surely
    you are dead, for I feel a little bit

dead myself. I'm feeble as an orphan.
    Still, your clocks twitch bravely forward, secondly

surviving. They mean well, but they do not
    help. Tomorrow is for sleeping late,

for thank-you cards, for day-old cake. Tomorrow,
    we will fill the dormant, dominant

hours with the mess of business that death
    brokers, the sole intent of which, I guess,

is to keep our forlorn hands engaged.
    On top of the buffet, a stack of paper

plates seem genuinely white as snow.
    This does little to console. Even so,

I seem committed to the ease by which
    they're nesting, with what palatable peace

they rest in. They do not thrash or wail
    or rend their clothes. This dinnerware is meant

to be disposed. Nobody wastes their tears
    on trash-bins heaped with half-eaten helpings

of food. Surely you're dead.
    We buried you.

buried

No father made profession of love.
No nurse called out for the doctor.
No teacher ate his apple,
Nor any binomial theories taught.

No saint discarded his tunic.
No indigent spied a good meal and took it.
No tunnel was carved into the wall of rock.
No honey was gathered, no honey was left to be gathered.

Never did a television turn us on.
No war was won, if ever one was fought.
There was no sleep, even as I tried it
To the heartbeat I inferred as Heaven's.

The blood was of no consequence without the cup
To carry it. No holy book of answers held the truth.
No god discovered me, smiling.
No smiling god will ever be discovered.

hotel infinity
In my Father's house are many mansions...
John 14:2

Shall I procure a room for us, or me alone?
    Who knows who I'll be doing when the trumpet blows

and the grand last call is bellowed from wherever Heaven
    deems to be, and every good spirit shouts *Land of Canaan*

Here I Come! Do I need to make a reservation?
    Could be quite the scandal, *hmm*? Who shall be forsaken

and who shall be redeemed? Not a saint will know
    until the time to die arrives then *off we go*

to a far and unseen planet where all rooms face east.
    That, so when we wake to death we are, at the very least,

fortified, eager to rise, rise with the sun and every angel
    batting wings against the light's auspicious swell,

oh conundrum city. What if I can't manage underneath the feathers?
    Worse, what if I'm unwelcome there, like hurricane weather

on the sheen, glass sands of Paradise's beach? *I cannot worry details*
    just this now. I've luggage to pack, the mail

to put on hold, and then to lay up treasure starting at this moment.
    With luck, this new wine pressed *vintage me* will ferment

into something good and grain.
    It is the tale of the chaff and the wheat again,

some to keep, and some to throw off to the birds, away.
    Until, I wait ready as virgins are for the day

when Jesus' very brawny arms will hold us.
    If it were not so—*wouldn't he have told us?*

threnody

The darkness mumbled *earthquake* and I could not help but go.
Under that black weakness, I couch against my soul

(or what is left of it beneath the rubble and the moan).
Grief remits to eulogize the whimper in my bones

and I am painful as the ache of open wounds
and their disease. But dying comes more soon

than I can beg it not to venture. It is not good,
this scheming anguish, unknown even to God,

so it seems. Some nights I think I see it in the fret
of my own eyes singed with sad fire, a last regret

still regretting herself. If I could be certain the prize
of death is paradise I might organize a belief to ease

me through *these hours,* extending so vastly that infinite
threads could be woven of their rending. But

I'm as far from *sure* as sea from shore.
Still, my prayer is pure.

a wish

A night so scarred
by lovers and their scars,
from the deep of a well
there are stars

but they are black
and they've been broken
so. I am blessed by the rude,
crude hand of a priest, beholden

now to him as night
feasts its fill
upon my ghost self. Yet I hold to it
jealously, *sour pill*.

For the crave of what my marrow's
left, I pray you get here God. Damn
or save what's sacred
of this soul (if at all you can

or if you dare to test
a Jesus love upon me). Until—
let the wish of it comfort me
atop this ash-hill.

houses, haunted

First House: The vacuum
      cinch of my mother's womb.

Second House: A trailer.
      Third House: Don't remember.

Fourth House: Fawnwood Road.
      Fifth House: Episodes

of feeling very, very poorly begin
      to show. *Sixth House:* I discipline

myself to these installments.
      Seventh House: An apartment,

collegiate. *Eighth House:*
      I grow mouse-

minuscule and eat only from traps.
      Ninth House: I strap

my body into the first of these
      wife-suits, clumsily.

Tenth House: A house of assignation.
      Eleventh House: Bourbon

Lake, enough to bathe in. *Twelfth*
      House: Thy rod and staff

comfort me, o Shepherd, but
      the footage of the room, cubits

only. *House Thirteen:* Seemed like a good
      idea at the time. I knocked its wooden

walls to keep the devil outside.
      Fourteenth House: I bride

again, but wisely.
      Fifteen: The house wherein I die by proxy,

Father in his hospital gown.
    Sixteen: The ingrown

dwelling of an anchoress.
    I hole up like an abscess

and I weep. *Seventeenth House:* I live in tents
    as the nomads do, intensely

ill-at-ease in stillness.
    Last House: A silence

crawls through me like a termite.
    The doorsill's sealed. Airtight.

a good christian mustn't fear the darkness of the grave

But let me tell you about its landscape. Small, hot, wooden,
and from above no one will hear you murmur *let me out.*
Out of the darkness nothing's delivered. Still, you beg it

to the brass of the coffin's creak hinge while satin
grows stench and your death dress rots away. You are livid
and left alone. The red jasper chaplet in your hand inclines

to the pretense of prayer. You are appalled, shrouded,
sutured shut. They did not put the pillow in between
your knees. And, your lipstick's smeared. *Once upon,*

you wished a thousand infinities. Finally arrived,
nothing can be more broken, nothing can be more
than dead. To the uncarved side of your stone,

a devil tree bends. But this, of course, is not the end.

the second day

They wandered in the wilderness in a solitary way;
they found no city to dwell in.
Psalm 107:4

I was not in safety, neither had I rest, neither was I quiet;
yet trouble came.
Job 3:26

on the second day

He descended into Hell, into what he thought
was Hell. He descended into himself. Prisoned
by the darkness there was nothing he could do, no
body left to see him through. He counted on his wounds
(*five all*), each pooled and bluing between the spices and the sheets,
as God had blessed him *bruisely*, in the manner of meat
unfit for priests, though keen for the fire. Oh, he was tired.
But the room knew him, wouldn't let him sleep. He tried
counting sheep, but Mary's little lamb had uttered not a *baa*
before the wolf screwed down his vise-box jaw
and the Agnus Dei caught her crook in the fence.
Nothing made sense, and no one came to save him.
The worms passed out psalters as the flies congregated.
So he prayed to the maggots and he waited.

epitaph

Night noises, mostly. Crickets and a siren,
the batting of prayers against a creosote,
the strum of branches scraping a wood fence,
the hush of my flush twin lips, entreating:
Dead should be quieter than this.
The black dove growls at my offense. So

there is nothing silent in any world. Not sleep,
not love, not Christ (who, on the very eve
of the fortieth day, sang like a sailor to the desert),
and Death, though she slinks about with the calm
of only the most skilled of shadowy men,
it is her rustle that gives her away:

such breath as the moon expires, under which
the soul of every weak thing dreams.

vesper

Breath on the window where frost has raped the sill—
be still, be still —

and I *am* still, still as a cavity, a lung or a vacant trunk,
hushed and drunk

on air and nothing but, and still I have not slept.
Though sleep has wept

for me a thousand times this year, each eye puckers ingenuine
tears, and even

rain makes little sense tonight, a faint, dark
noise, one half of a bark

from the throat of a moon-mad dog stalking the bed.
Is it better to be dead

or dying? I am tacked into place with sewing pins,
unmoved, thin

and hungry for the lids to slip and fall. Winter
burns me to a shiver

and I am unlucky this way—for night to wait hovering
until the edge of day, unrecovering.

danse macabre

Weep off that white dress, My Insomniac.
It's *mourning* and I've come to spirit you
away. Don't cry. I'll do it quietly
and clean. You will not feel a thing, neither
spasm nor shard, as I tap to the siphon
of your wee, wet heart and bleed your vain veins dry.
I'll prop your head on your fist in a dis-tressed pose,
so all will know it was not willingly
you went, and in that way, the virtues you
brood prudely maiden on. My nectarine,
I'll pare by halves your berry. *Taste and see.*
For in this world you are not meant to feel
so safe. As for the next, its own suspense
contends. Besides, there's no true thrill in love
until you're done by someone dangerous.
So leave the happy, harmless boys to rot,
and open now your dead and darling arms.
I'll prove the mysteries of eternal life.
How wide they stretch the pleat of your delight.
Babe. I'm with you always. *Just like Christ.*

what we didn't

As the bastard daughter of the Holy Ghost,
no birthright saved me. No inheritance, no land.
You thought that was more than a little funny,
a curious kind of queer, remarkable as souls
in Purgatory and the dubious question
of their redemption. We never cleared that up.
We didn't manage to get past. Now I am here,
empty of flesh as a skeleton and lacking a face.
We had no child named Epic. We did not bother
to bequest. There are memories in the garden,
but the gate's quite locked, quite tightly.
A sublingual bitterness savages—*let not this pain
be so present*. Dead, it seems, is a difference
of opinion. And now I wait.

the lord summons his regret

Valley, grow tall like the mountain is.
Crocus, bloom from a rocky place.
Lamb, bleat meanly a hymn of strangeness.
Thunder, rain fire and forty days.

Sun, quaver your shine into silence.
Chokecherry tree, bear only dire fruit.
Husband, unlace your mistress' bodice.
Woman, make meal of it, leaf to root.

Prophet, loose the knot of your sandal.
Murderer, pray to my clemency.
Flax-matron, toss off the rod and spindle.
Savior, recall your Calvary.

Jupiter, arc a final orbit.
Priest, enflesh the wine and the bread.
Daughter, compose your mother's obit.
Bridegroom, rapture the maidenhead.

Paraclete, flame from the mouths of sinners.
Body, prepare to rise from the grave.
Magdalene, let down your hair and come hither.
Gabriel, take up your trumpet and *rage*.

new jerusalem

In the crook arm of a shadow left by light to guard this temple,
it is either noon or three a.m. The hour is equivalent.
No matter, chimes the little bird, his thirteen even appeals.

Drear with envy, a new earth erupts. The sign points only
to itself. A city screams its infancy. Pure gold, brittle,
transparent as glass and alchemized.

It thirsts for the sea and for all things swimming it. Beckoning,
the ninth suckered tentacle of the cephalopod's sorrow *(believe
it)*. Regret, I am to learn, is a fisherman's net. Hunger,

the haunt of the Holy Spirit as she starves. I make a martyr's
cross upon my breasts. Wasn't I meant for this?
Surely Jesus is doomed to arrive.

What takes the place of sleep for the walking or the dead?
Mornings come closest to it, a flustered early peace called dawn,
and someone moving unseen as the stark darkness

rises. Babylon's whore, she goes as a mistress goes, only
on her knees, but beautifully dressed, willing as no wife.
Could I close my eyes, this would be the dream I urged and reeled to.

a razor to the throat ought to do it—
> *Anyone here had a go at themselves / for a laugh?*
> "I Say I Say I Say" Simon Armitage

but if a blood oath's not your wrecking pleasure,
        give *this* sassy trick a spin: Lay your body down

upon the goosefeather bed and just *pretend* that you are
        dead. It's worked before, *oh hasn't it?* Suffer

your eyes shut tight as a lock-box, lest any mystery
        grief slip out. Do you doubt that you can do it?

Try talking yourself through it. With conviction
        to befit the desperately diseased, recite your plan

to the mattress springs: *Breath, be held in the flinch*
        of these wrists, for you squirm from my grip

like a kitten. Close enough for hand grenades,
        or the ravel of the hangman's noose, which—*shall I*

remind you?—slipped loose from the fist of your head
        like a misthrown punch. *Some luck.* Now, plug

your throat with a well-poisoned plum. You'll perish
        seven deaths while you're waiting for the Prince.

He never comes to kiss it out. That dim, grim, bother
        of a rib. *Piss on him.* You're best off alone.

You shall star in a Single-Woman Show. Act One,
        Disappearing Do. Bow to your own, grand rounds

of applause. Did I say rounds? You could manage
        by a solitary bullet. They'll putty up your skull

with plaster. What a laugh. *Quel Disastre!* You'll take
        the very cake away. Your famous face will proceed

the parade. You will be saved. And no one ought feel
        smug enough to blame you. Neither will they call you

by your given name, *Queen Bee.* You can hive out
        the span of your rotting spree in a golden tomb,

a Drone (not unlike the other ones) to comb through
        the honey of your tears. That could take years,

conceivably. But to that end, God promises
        a pretty room in which to wait. A nice place,

really. Quiet, if a tad sight cramped and chilly.
        Remarkable, though. All roses and balloons.

Truly, it should swoon you to it, blissfully senseless, drunk
        as if you've swigged it from the oven's hissing whisper.

Swell touch, if your note is cryptically composed.
        Suchlike your own brief life, it's left for the scholars

to somehow surmise. How bravely you held on
        until finally—*you died*—

in your sad little bed on that trash of a night.
        But you're simply pretending. *Right?*

gethsemane

There are demons who have left their homes,
dead men who sleep with bones and distorted men,
the bodies of weak men grown shoddy in their sleep.
Let *them* pray the Lord's Prayer daily, *foolish sheep*.

Then it is the moon ascending to a place called God,
though when she gets there, no one's left to praise.
Take to your knee and get it over with.
Oh miracle is often more than this.

In huddles we war and we rumor of war,
while *monk* means solitude in Greek or something like it.
I should be a winter bride next time, if I am able.
White, all cold as the devil.

a little song

Prayers might succor the dead,
but gifts laid at the gravehead

will go to vultures blunt and blackheart
enough to fathom that they aren't

on their ways to dying, too.
So smirks me, from this tiny, pine room.

postmark from gehenna

Something in me warned of this. Here, the land
will not let alone. From the Rift Valley
to the Sea of Salt and beyond, I look
for your hands to place mine into. *Have I
forgotten to bring them?* They were denied
me. *The body dies and takes us with it.*
A bird at the helm of a weatherwood branch
moves in twitches. She is tiny and severe.
She watches me, I think, her black eyes conjecting
*will she manage when the winter comes, as it does
even here?* At my feet, there are markings,
serpentine furrows in the ground. Perhaps
I am being followed. Do not doubt it.

It is a dark place. *A very dark place.*

what (c)remains
for my mother

Her skin, her wrists, her fists, her shins—
    the plan of her hands, the remnants of them. But how,

Sir, did she burn? Did she flash out like a star?
    Sear like a roast? Did she flame up with panache,

or was it all and simply pain? Promise again:
    Only her body is over, is done. Her soul (so you've told), is

someplace keen and green. I can't say I'm convinced.
    Cold Ghost, have you spun her into gold? The filaments,

the bits left singeing from the old retort? *A harmless fact*
    of absence. Nothing more, nothing less. I envy the urn

that holds her, but only because it can. Her flesh is finished.
    Her knees, their kneeling complete. The heart's been leached

of love. But did she suffer much? Did she smolder? *Oh*
    only her body is over. Are all of her pieces resting in peace?

The ground down bones, the shards that were her arms?
    Did she blister? Did she bleed? *Never you mind it. She is*

released. Christ, go comfort someone else. You crawled
    from the tomb like getting out of bed. You did not stay dead.

Your last breath wasn't. And I don't think that's very fair.
    Forgive me if you must or if you dare. *Ashes to dust*

or despair, I suppose. Did the char come first,
    or did the blaze? Defend, Oh God, your ways,

your meaner means. How exactly has your will been done?
    And where, *precisely*, has she gone?

an alabaster jar and its oil

Broken open, Jesus will be finished too, bled out
like spiced perfume upon a woman's hands. Years
will pass, and still it will be only the faint waft of Christ
that I sense in the attic, in the stars, in this mortal form
his body assumes beside me. The poor are with us
everywhere and always. Sickness coughs and cries
under blankets, bridges. Daily, inner Pharisees
rebuke me when all I desire is to weep upon his feet,
to eager the hazards of his cheek, to read to the rim
of his lip, the scroll of my hair. It is not the shattered jar
but the oil inside. Everything that bleeds or leaks from us
shall be recovered in a moment hereafter. That is
a promise I dare at once to doubt and to believe. Oh
God, if we touch (but for a moment) will you know me?

once was i

a person, now I am no longer—
but I made anyway of myself
a lover to you. My ghostliness

wore a crown of rue and daisies
at the amber coast, where darkness
comes sooner. A Latvian's heart for Luther,

my soul was in a Baltic state, ravaged,
dead and cold and sad. I left open
the gates to the tomb. I hoped you'd steal a relic,

a kneecap to remind you exactly
how well I knelt, how lovely I looked
from above. When you didn't dare,

I moved through you, listening
for the aspirate h in *ah,* feeling
with the phantom of my hands

for the quivering Braille of gooseflesh
underneath your belly. Nothing came
but darkness, itself raptly

inattentive. What noise but an unheard
rustle when she whispers, a woman whose lips
are so numb? *Burned,* even?

a funerary catechism

Who is God? *Somebody, somewhere.*
      Where does He live? *Not here.*

Where did you come from? *Disbelief.*
      Where are you going? *Beneath.*

What is the soul? *A very grave thing.*
      And what is the body? *Nothing.*

What is Original Sin? *Debatable.*
      The nature of man? *He's feeble.*

Who is Christ? *A guy on a cross.*
      What did he do? *He lost.*

What is The Spirit? *The ghost of a chance.*
      How does She help you? *She can't.*

And what is the sum of dead and forever?
      It's never.

the question is one of ashes and dust

It is not my name, which you have already
inked into one interminable book or the other. Also,
not what virtue I've claimed to store up

in two unrelenting fists. Also, not the hands
which wrap around them, these hands
from which I feed, strong though they are,

but defiled. On the Eve of the End of it All,
it is only this: how my lips catch fire,
how I burn *exactly*, an effigy in my heart, awful

as an offering. How the darkness blesses its shadow
as the indigent lauds his begging bridge. How like a virgin
I've trimmed my wick. How well I can wrestle

your mystery to the ground, Angry Angel.
How I blunt my feathers on the blade of your tooth.
How I bleed like Christ through the white of my dress,

my fingers so steady, so stained.

as one crying out in the wilderness

It was a voice I thought I heard.
        I swore to make straight the way of the Lord,

and the altar gave a little quiver.
        I licked the cup of wine as if it were a lover's

lip, while the angled face of an acolyte
        bent into a genuflecting scowl. That night,

the transept swayed and flailed
        like the grown, pale

arms of a woman waving goodbye.
        I was drunk and high,

though neither were enough to soothe
        me into sleep. My tooth

hurt like fair warning.
        My face was raped redly, burning

as a book might, were it a sign.
        All the eve long, I pried

at my shut soul with the lock pick of a prayer.
        God, fretted I, *if you are there,*

then you must now answer,
        one way or another.

But only the candle blinked.
        So I took another drink.

He discovereth deep things out of darkness, and bringeth out to light the shadow of death.
Job 12:22

And the serpent cast out of his mouth water as a flood after the woman, that he might cause her to be carried away of the flood.
Revelation 12:15

on the third day

He rose again. His face was black and bruised.
The underground famine had gnawed its gloss.
Where I have been, you could not live to tell.
First, his women returned, and then his friends.
They reached to press their fingers to his scar.
Do not touch me, he scolded crossly, cold
as Christ. Instead, they stroked the air, feeling
by degree for what had changed. But new moods
bloomed from his skin and from his bristle.
He spit upon the ground and then he cursed.
He did not walk towards the light, he walked
away. And the lock-jaw mouth of the grave
stayed agape, misgiving. As if it did
not know: *Dead does not mean dead forever.*

variety of hells

> *Hell: the inescapable presence of God*
> *endured in the permanent absence of Him.*

A hell where your name is forgotten.
Worse, the hell that remembers you.
Every rotten scheme your hands laid plan to.

Then, a hell for omissive sins.
All what you meant to do though couldn't.
How you intended to love, but didn't.

A hell for revenge songs and ridicule.
A hell where despair is winnowed by fire.
A hell that burns away desire.

Hell of all hells: I harrow for your ghost.
But we abide eternities apart.
That's the hell of the heart.

what death makes of you

You'll seem somehow shorter for awhile to come:
       hyperbarically compressed, a Styrofoam cup

in a pressurized box, your body's blue balloon
       grown small, all your high, hot air forced through.

And you will seem unfocused for a woe's
       worth of seasons. Blurred like a badly posed

photograph, others will squint to make you out.
       It weren't my fault, you'll duly announce.

The subject moved. I guess I snapped. Truly,
       the subject did move. The subject moved to a far-away

place. He changed his name and did not leave
       a forwarding address. He moved without heaving

a muscle. He moved sans shoes and *sans souci.*
       The subject moved away from thee. That's the mystery.

Where one flees to when he's over is anyone's best
       guess. What death makes of you is, simply, a mess.

And, it's no matter whether you're the griever or the one
       who's grieved. You're stiff, stifled, stalled. You're alone,

you're cold, and you haven't any real thing you can do
       with the time you're biding but brood

through it. You're sewn all shut and your heart's
       been removed. A midnight stroll through the churchyard

yields no tangible results. Hand it to God, keeping
       the dead so non-demurring. Speaking

of hands, you're likely to forget exactly where
       yours are supposed to go and how they are

to do. And who. Reach to the comfort of otherflesh,
       its feel against your palms will shudder you to fresh

despair. He who was *here* is now *there*, wherever
       there is and goddamn if you know. Be you a believer,

perhaps you'll pray for your relief. Maybe you'll get
       it. Or maybe you'll resign to wrap up in a blanket

of your own boohooing and let the telephone trill and trill on.
       There'll be nothing you want more than to also be gone.

For, in the age it takes a condolence rose to wilt,
       what's hope in you will also be killed.

Who's to say if it will rise? Not much
       separates the living from the not-alive. Each

is sentenced to a same and sorry fate:
       Six feet of silt. A name. Two dates.

But rest you easy. This won't happen for a long and lusty
       span of years. For now, consider the lilies.

Toil-less and unspinning, they do not seem to trouble
       over what's to pass. Yea, though you rubble

through the Valley of Alas, may you dread neither flower nor
       final farewell. Unwind with a Scotch or two or four

or seven. Drunk is a little like heaven. Glory
       (or *Glenfiddich*) be. Let not the cup pass. Your misery

is yours alone. The only true thing you'll ever outright
       own. And know—you've been transfigured, sure as Christ.

O Glorious Splendor, let your face shine on like the moon's
       black side. You are atop a mountain,

keening with the spirits of saints, and your friends,
       though sympathetic, cannot comprehend

what's changed. In your condition, they suppose
       you're either mad or ghost. And death has made you both.

an ache like a stone

Every Christian mystery sounds like nonsense:
the God who is one and three, the bread that is not bread,
how, three days suppressed, the unearthed Jesus gleamed
like pirate bounty, his chest full of gold and a hook in his hand.

The center of anything is safest. Though I move horizontally,
a strong calm secures me, an exhausted door locks.
For the marriage of Hosanna to Regret, I hold the palm aloft.
It is a green victory in my fist.

Woman, why do you weep? I confess each tear is its own.
They tribute the dying I will someday do, how I will travel
atop the brawn back of an ass to one Jerusalem or another,
and how I will do it aching like a stone, dead and done,

but glorified, *glorified*. There, I'll find fresh crosses
and a blood knot leaching through a veil. Sodden yet flourishing,
it is the headdress of queenly triumph, my ragged reward.
Oh how I shall wear it like a wound.

these last things (lest i forget them)

A beautiful woman softens my passing.
I remove my name and my coat. Wise
and very warm, she gives me the blessing
I ask for. It is written on a stone
and it heavies me to carry it, like a secret.

Then she is gone. I come to the garden
alone. When the white rose purrs for me
to touch it, I lay what is left of my fingers
upon the bare bone of its thorn, testing my virtue
against its victory. The dew on the bud

undoes me. What happens next comes quickly,
quietly: a castle, a ceremony, a sharp, red ring.
He is tall as a king, and yet more kingly.
The clothes fall away from my body
and I shame only over my shivering.

And he takes me to an island in the ocean,
bringing to my lips a fig of exquisite
serenity, rare and ripe. Undulations occur.
Above us, the moon seems different,
uneclipsed and in another sky. And the water

braces itself against the waves we make. And dark
inside the safety of the sea, there are creatures,
rapt and ravenous. And the sky is filled with anthem
and albatross as his hands delight over me.
We come like the clouds of heaven.

cross

The branches of this tree
not broken, not bent —
but *spent*.

And no amount of tears
might drown the vacant
hole that rants

into hell. Three days, and
a sleep so catastrophically scarred
that nightmares mar

even the living landscape.
Who will rest in the City of Bread?
Soon, soon. The head's

already in the sky. Mercy
on the splinter and the thorn.
To die is to be born.

la petite mort

We who cannot sleep for brooding over
each other, whose hands roam the coasts of our
bodies like trawlers pearling for oysters,
and under whose plain, predestined hungers
these sweltering hours have nursed, we've come
to the end, yet again. The pleasure's done.
Our child, she died between us, unctioned,
confessed, naked before her gods. With bedroom
grief, we nursed those final aches, we tinctured
her with opiates to soothe her pain. Cure
of absolute cures, we tied a ligature
of leeches to our lips and bled her
dry as a white bone. Only the winding
sheet knows how deep the wound goes. Morning,
we'll summon to the garden her weakling
corpse to grieve. Christ, have mercy on this being,
who rose up despite that divine bargain
of human finitude. And may she live again—
another night—in the manner of the chronic moon,
who never truly dies, but coxswains
through the night sky's sea, eternally begun
each month, body reborn. We beg it to be done.
For sex is the solvent of all isolation,
a prayer invoked in tears, spoken in tongues.

cinerary song

> *For, behold, the day cometh, that shall burn as an oven...*
> Malachi 4:1

This is the furnace
where bones come down to burn.
Love, it's your turn.

Bliss of my bliss,
like Apples of Sodom
your hands turn to ash as I hold them

and neither root nor branch
remains of your tree.
Your limbs — *mere effigies* —

blaze on. All what you were
is done. The grave
holds its own flesh coldly. Days,

even years will pass
and I will remember only this:
the silent treble in your voice

when I told your body goodbye.
But heaven's no home for despair.
Soon, you'll be free as air.

the things they don't tell you about heaven

Apples still taste like apples. Funny thing,
serpents taste like apples too, and kisses
and bread. In fact, it is all about apples,
this place. Everything you touch is smooth and red.
Your skin is comfortably heavy on your bones,
like that sleepy moment between being awake and falling
into a dream. The moon is a pendulum clock,
and light from the sun comes down in drops, as rain. And,
as any child will tell you, what we call rain is really tears,
the soul of God weeping over something great or small,
as anything with a soul will do from time to time.
Mostly, it is the apples, and a longing kind of sad.
They are firm as musculature. They smell like the flesh
and juice of unrequited love.

says some angel to one mary or another—

Not in the garden, not in the tomb,
not in the old shoe. Not in the furnace,
its resonance and heat. The telephone's signature

ring is silent now, no voice to carouse the tenor
and tremble of righter dreams. The rosebuds have
a clean finger to their lips—*hush*. He is not in the second hand,

which ticks upon itself. *Hush*—he's not in the second chance,
that old hope which stumbles like a nomad over the Reed Sea.
Indeed, the cellar door is locked and nothing sweet inside

but the perverse perseverance of jelly jars, red, wet cherries
from a spinster's finest branch. Taste and see: He's not
in the swallow, the tongue or the teeth. No one such as you desire,

here today. Oh Lady, look to otherwise, turn to Oz or Elsewhere,
juncture of M and 12 on a fantasized map. The he you seek
might shroud out upon an island for years and songs

under the perils of a kiss beneath an uncharted chair.
Or, open your palm to cradle something small and dear.
Perhaps he's there.

mount

I am in a graveyard, weeping out the drone
        of a crude song I ought better sing alone —

yet I rude it aloud to an audience of pities.
        Authored in the stone carver's art, full cities

of death spill before me as a maze
        and I maneuver them, myrrhing through the haze

of incense left behind from last night's vespers
        and the burial. Between the coiffured

flowers and the widowly weeping, the priest's
        plea continues: *Lord, into thy mansions, receive.*

What of this world is welcomed
        into the next? A pigeon's

wing blinks across a Mary's marble eye.
        I brave it to the new tomb: *I*

must be assured that God lets us remember.
        Once, at the web and juncture of my fingers,

it was the wax of a thin man's candle, the glorious
        tree of his cock. He said *your dress*

is beautiful (having me at that). I radiated for thrilling
        days, the cloth, blue and pooling

at the ache of our Achilles as he tore
        should from my *shoulder. Lover,*

come down here to me, he betrothed.
        With what deliberation, still another rose

from his chair when the gray room's light leisured
        over my entrance. His veins traced maps of pleasure

from the knuckles of his finger to the downy rise
    where spread the butter of my thigh

upon the bread of his hip. But I am with a cemetery's
    envy. The crosses are creeping stiffly

up the hill. I gave the dress to charity.
    Truth: *All seams eventually*

unravel. Another: *We inter the dead, forgetting*
    that dead people are people yet (though rotting)

and everyone will one day rise. The stone carver took
    a woman to his bed. Naked, she looked

like a seraph or a snake. He invented her
    into the details of the sepulcher,

a round face beaming resurrective glee
    to the unknown body hollowing beneath.

Nothing is silly if you love it. The crypts
    proclaim this in their postscript —

Beloved Father. Until the Angels Come.
    She Never Walked Alone.

What's buried only seems asleep. Truth: *Under the tumulus*
    are dreams untold. From a graveyard, Jesus

got up and walked away, having courage
    such as someone who is stranger to this earth, the dotage

of Magdalene reaching up from the mud
    while he left his shroud at her knees. God,

I *do* remember reaching up. You tied my neck
    into your tunic. You lugged me, trailing, like a sack.

The stone carver's mistress died last year.
    Ferns and pale lilies were burned upon her bier

and the smoke of it blackened everyone's
    face. In a graveyard I remember the dying I've done,

the dying I'll do. Desire is an appetite,
    a mere full plum and its plumpness, white

as an ice-floe in the cold wild of raw and cringing.
    I remember the invisible twinge

in your groin I did not see but knew as it was leaping.
    I remember the kiss of it, groping

up towards the shim of your saddle. Bliss
    is indeed a kind of death, and possible. Christ

will die, rise, and die again, for as many Sundays
    as the world has left but I will lay out all body

for the anguish of my holy self's howl
    against the scheme of anyone's scowl

eye or even the mercy of God's own mother.
    I remember the cruciform pose of you, who shuddered

above me. We prayed. We fucked. We confessed.
    We chorused to the hymn: *Oh beautiful, beautiful dress.*

rsvp

No, no, no.
I will not go.
Death can wait
its long, late
time away,
placing daisies
on someone else's grave.

I am off to elsewhere.
Let the devil share
his dram and groan
with another body's bones.
And even Heaven
(a place far better than regret)
can't have me yet.

if we meet again

I will tell you finally that every star searched out
with science's telescopic eye (even the luckiest,
flaring brightly against the Hunter's cleft), is no more
a star than I am. They are all dead, each of them expired.

Because, there is no true knowledge we can have
of anything *light*. Not of the universe,
not of each other. We must endure
as afterthought the brilliance that we bore.

For even if we held ourselves tight as sisters,
there would be infinities of points between the seams
where our skins met, or tried to. This is why it feels
as if we've never touched. Still,

I will to you my genuflecting rose, parched but yet inclining
to submit her petal to your pleasure. And the memoir,
into which I spelled our names with a martyr's alphabet,
a for *almost, be* for *was* —

Keep my cherished spyglass. Through it,
we watched whole galaxies heave, come,
then go. If we meet again, I will tell you nothing
was as sweet as that. Nothing ever will be.

the naming of things

If in the aftermath of heaven
there is anything left standing and gold,
would I be so brave as to bring it to you, and
from such rubble could we ever *be?*

And after death's reminiscing shadow passes over
the afternoon of all things living,
will it be *at last* that we are called
by our own, our true names?

Not the ones our mothers gave us,
hardly knowing yet what we would come to mean,
but those syllables that we can only utter in silence:
a gaze just exactly the width of my thumb,

the meter and sonnet of your breath.

deathday

Infinities wiser than right this now,
        in a far and other time ahead.
        The unfeeling stare the mirror dreads
will no longer *be:* Brow

having done with her brooding
        will be done with herself, and the body
        retreats in refuge. Dare say what glory
awaits the perished, the concluding?

This, the last
        of all living days. Expect to see
        in the ligature of the Madonna Lily's
new-bloomed buds, a vast

elliptical otherwise floating
        tight and high above their stems,
        those dear, damn blossoms of regret. When
comes that day, prize the utmost

aberrations of the sun's peculiar light—
        an airglow, a luminosity, the cloudy
        inclination of forever to be.
Oh Insomniac, death will arrive

like sleep—the alpine thrum
        of the icy, unfamiliar gaze
        that was my face,
but finally calm.

last day

And shall I rise up
like a loaf of bread
from being *so dead?*

Should I walk
towards the light,
or is it a trick *(consider*

the wick of the candle,
the very poor moth winging
into its flame)? Will my name

suffice itself, a good deed,
done? And how will You
re-member me, knitting

once again my limbs to my skin?
I shall be quite new,
if You please it. Is there room

enough for everyone?
And will it be any fun? Or,
will we reverence ourselves

into eternal ennui? Will the guilty
be gleefully redeemed, or are only
the holy made whole? Tell me,

what exactly will flash before my face
that day—the sum of all my sins,
or the figure of Your perfect grace?

o afterwards: **a benediction**

And may the old life, that rotting flesh and treasure,
find in the good pleasure

of Christ, a forgetfulness complete: that these sins, however
humanly deliberate my misbehaviors,

be blotted from the record of God, raptured like the night's thief,
forever gone, newly clean.

And may this new self shine like the moon shone long ago, before
she was rent by the devil's incisor,

a whole, round body not meant to be broken into phases.
And may she sing your praises

like Golgotha sings of a tree: for there is nothing empty
that cannot be filled. And may the sea

and all things swimming it thirst no longer for Living Water.
And may the Father

know the Daughter, even as the end of the earth unfolds.
And may I turn to gold.

Acknowledgements

Sincere gratitude to the publications in which these poems originally appeared:

Agenda: "Surely You're Dead, We Eulogized you"; *Borderlands:* "Early Morning Prayer"; *The Christian Century:* "A Good Christian Mustn't Fear the Darkness of the Grave," "Cross," "O Afterwards: A Benediction," "Says some angel to one Mary or another—," "Varieties of Hell," "The Question is One of Ashes and Dust," and "On the Third Day"; *Christianity and Literature:* "On the First Day"; *Concordia English Journal:* "What (C)remains," "RSVP," "The Naming of Things"; *Drunken Boat:* "The Great Undertaking"; *High Plains Literary Review:* "Vesper"; *The Langdon Review:* "What We Did," "What We Didn't," "On the Second Day"; *The Lucid Stone:* "Gethsemane"; *No Tell Motel:* "As One Crying Out in the Wilderness," "A Razor to the Throat Ought to Do It"; *Phoenix Rising:* "Cemetery Road," "Hotel Infinity," "Threnody"; *Rhino:* "Houses, Haunted"; *Sojourners:* "Last Day," "The things they don't tell you about heaven"; *Word For/Word:* "Necropolis."

"An Alabaster Jar and Its Oil" was written for a chapel service at the Episcopal Theological Seminary of the Southwest

"As One Crying Out in the Wilderness," "Last Day," The Question is One of Ashes and Dust" and "The Lord has Summoned His Regret" were written as part of an ongoing tithe of poems to First English Lutheran Church, Austin, TX.

Special thanks to the following poets for their advice and support during this project: Craig Arnold, Jill Baumgaertner, Bruce Covey, Lyman Grant, Reb Livingston, Jessica Piazza, Louisa Spaventa, Larry Thomas.

Exceptional thanks are due to the magnificent Neil Ellis Orts, my ever-patient editor.

I also want to acknowledge my parents. I love and miss them dearly.

Jim Schulz
1942-1999

Ann Schulz-Hale
1942-2004